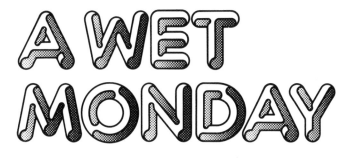

A WET MONDAY

DOROTHY EDWARDS
AND JENNY WILLIAMS

WILLIAM MORROW AND COMPANY
NEW YORK 1976

Published in the United States in 1976.
Text copyright © 1975 by Dorothy Edwards
Illustrations copyright © 1975 by Jenny Williams
Published in Great Britain in 1975.
Printed in the United States of America.
1 2 3 4 5 80 79 78 77 76

Library of Congress Cataloging in Publication Data

Edwards, Dorothy.
  A wet Monday.

  SUMMARY: On one particular rainy Monday, all the members of a family have a difficult day.
  [1. Rain and rainfall—Fiction.   2. Family life—Fiction]
I. Williams, Jenny, 1939-   II. Title.
PZ7.E2518We   [E]   76-12405
ISBN 0-688-32081-3 lib. bdg.
ISBN 0-688-27081-6 pbk.

Monday again.
Look at it.
Look at it.
Rain, rain, rain.

Mom's fed up.
Dad's fed up.
Tracy's fed up.
I'm fed up.
Toby's fed up.
What a day.

On and on.
Nag, nag, nag.
Where's Mom's key?
Where's Dad's cap?
Where's Tracy's cape?
Where's my bag?
Where's Toby's dish?
What a day.

Drip, drip, drip.
Nag, nag, nag.
Mom yells at Dad.
Dad yells at Tracy.
Tracy yells at me.
I yell at Toby.
Toby goes to his box.
What a day.

Rain, rain, rain.
Splash, splash, splash.
Dad's late for work.
I'm late for school.
Tracy's late for nursery school.
Mom's *very* late for work.
And Toby's not been out.
What a day.

Rain, rain, rain.
Mom's boss is mad.
Dad hits his hand.
Tracy will not play.
I hit a boy.
Toby wets the floor.
What a day.

Drip, drip, drip.
Mom has a row.
Dad's hand is bad.
Tracy is told off.
The boy hits me.
Toby's back in bed.
What a day.

Mom storms out.
A nurse gets Dad tea.
Tracy is mad.
So is the boy, and so am I.
Toby tears Dad's paper.
What a day.

Mom gets Tracy;
they go home.
Dad sees the doctor;
he goes home.
The boy and I make up;
I go home.
Where is Toby?
What a mess.

There's Toby!
There he is!
Look what he's done!

Mom laughs.
Dad Laughs.
Tracy laughs.
I laugh.
Poor old Toby.
You never went out!

Come for a run, Toby.
Come for a run.
Mom will get tea.
The rain has gone.
See, the sun!
Run, run.
That was some day.